THE FRANKENBAGEL MONSTER

DANIEL PINKWATER

E. P. DUTTON   NEW YORK

Library of Congress Cataloging-in-Publication Data
Pinkwater, Daniel M., date
   The Frankenbagel monster.
   Summary: When a night-roaming monster is seen in
various sections of the city, few people suspect that
it is the creation of the local bagel maker, Harold
Frankenbagel.
   [1. Bagels—Fiction.   2. Monsters—Fiction.
3. Bakers and bakeries—Fiction.   4. Humorous stories]
I. Title.
PZ7.P6335Fr   1986   [E]   86-4608
ISBN 0-525-44260-X

Published in the United States by E.P. Dutton,
2 Park Avenue, New York, N.Y. 10016
a division of NAL Penguin Inc.
Published simultaneously in Canada by
Fitzhenry & Whiteside Limited, Toronto
Editor: Ann Durell   Designer: Edith T. Weinberg
Printed in Hong Kong by South China Printing Co.
First Edition   W   10 9 8 7 6 5 4 3 2

This book is
dedicated to the bagel,
friend of humankind
through the ages.

a newspaper clipping

"Bagels are my life," says Harold Frankenbagel, owner and operator of BAGEL MASTER of 3322 Blurpp Avenue. "In this business it's not enough to make a good bagel—you have to think like a bagel. I know what I'm talking."

Harold Frankenbagel is a popular figure in his neighborhood. His bagel shop is a favorite of many. Harold himself is well liked and friendly. On Sundays he makes miniature bagels and gives them to children who come to his shop. Everyone likes him and his bagels.

But late at night, when people are asleep, Harold Frankenbagel smiles a strange smile as he locks the door of his bagelworks. He drives to open-all-night bagel shops far across town—even to bagel shops in distant cities—places where he is not known. There he asks for unheard-of bagels: ice-cream bagels, celery-and-prune bagels, chicken-soup bagels, singing bagels, flying bagels, and electronic bageloids which are actually computers and can answer any question.

When the people in the bagel shops are unable to provide these strange bagels, Harold Frankenbagel smiles his secret smile. Then he goes back to his own bagelworks. Late at night, in the little room at the back of his shop, Harold Frankenbagel works on bagels never seen before. The room is full of strange, odd, unnatural things—like bagels, but not bagels—Harold Frankenbagel's failed experiments; also talking bagels, whirling bagels, Fourth-of-July fireworks bagels, and the incredible whirling–spinning–flying–talking–ice-cream–celery-prune–chicken-soup-computerized–exploding bagel, his greatest creation—except one...

the Glimville Bagelunculus, a huge bagel of im-
mense strength, capable of moving at the command
of its creator, Harold Frankenbagel.

Few people, if any, suspect that Harold Franken-bagel is actually the mad bagel maker of Glimville. Few people know of the ghastly thing he has cre-ated, which will be known to history as the Glimville Bagelunculus. Few people know of the madness of Harold Frankenbagel, which sends the bagel-thing lurching into the streets of Glimville at night, striking terror into the hearts of the populace—nor do peo-ple know precisely what manner of thing is spread-ing terror in the darkness. All that is known is that a night-roaming monster of some sort has been seen in various sections of the city.

Professor Sir Arnold Von Sweeney reads accounts of these strange events in the newspaper. "This is an interesting development," says the professor. "I shall look into it."

Professor Von Sweeney is an expert on many strange subjects. He has studied a number of supernatural events in which food has gone mad, including the Night-Stalking Celery of New Jersey, the Vampire Squash of Washington State, and the Chopped-Liver Devil which struck New Orleans in the late 1950s. Professor Von Sweeney suspects from certain signs that a very large and possibly evil bagel is loose in the streets of Glimville.

The professor appears in the shop of the mad bagel maker, Harold Frankenbagel. Frankenbagel denies that he knows anything about the monster— but he is worried. He has heard of Professor Von Sweeney, and he is afraid his monster will be discovered. Frankenbagel is not really bad. It is his insane desire to be the greatest bagel maker in history that has led him to create the unholy Bagelunculus.

Indeed, the bagel monster has done no real harm, other than to terrify a few late strollers. Until, one night, having gathered power from a bag of bright blue garlic carelessly left nearby, it comes awake all by itself, smashes through the wall of Harold Frankenbagel's shop, and lumbers off into the night.

Frankenbagel goes to Professor Von Sweeney's house. He confesses everything. He's frightened that the giant bagel monster will do some serious harm. He asks the professor to help him find and stop his horrible creation before it does some real damage.

They find the renegade bageloid trying to gain entrance to a lox warehouse. "Egad!" says Harold Frankenbagel. "What can this mean to the city of Glimville?"

"You should ask, What can this mean to civilization?" says Professor Von Sweeney. "If the monster gets to the thousands of pounds of incredibly nutritious lox stored in this warehouse, its powers will increase ten thousand times. Then it might become really grouchy and perhaps destroy Earth."

"What can we do?" Frankenbagel wails.

"There is only this," says the professor. "We must plan to eat the bagel monster for breakfast tomorrow."

"How can we possibly eat it? It's huge and evil!"

"We do not eat it—we *plan* to eat it! There's a difference. But you must join me in planning. Now, what do you say we eat that big bagel for breakfast, Harold?"

"I don't understand," says Frankenbagel.

"Just play along," whispers Professor Sir Arnold Von Sweeney.

"I get it," Harold Frankenbagel whispers back. "It sounds like a good idea to me. LET'S EAT THAT BIG BAGEL!"

"I think we should slice it in two and spread it with cream cheese and jelly. Do you agree?"

"Sure. That sounds fine. Shall we spread some butter on it too?"

"An excellent idea, Frankenbagel. And let's have some eggs on the side."

As the formerly mad (and now simply terrified) bagel maker and the great scientist discuss eating the gigantic bagel, the horrible thing itself is about to break into the loxworks. However, as they speak, its movements become slower and less violent. Soon it can hardly move.

"What's happening?" Frankenbagel shouts. "It seems to be slowing down."

"Naturally. It's going stale," says the learned Von Sweeney. "In a couple of days, it will be hard as a rock and no danger to anyone."

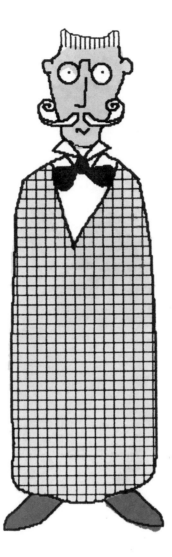

"But how did you know that it would go stale like that?"

"Just a matter of experience," says Professor Von Sweeney. "Bagels always go stale just before you're ready to eat them—everyone knows that. I simply assumed that this universal truth would apply to your monster bagel."

"How can I thank you, Professor Von Sweeney? You've saved mankind."

"Just learn a lesson from this and never again tamper with the unknown—and, especially, never again make a bagel more powerful than yourself."

"I promise, professor. I've learned my lesson."

Harold Frankenbagel and Professor Von Sweeney walk away in the first light of dawn. They are sober men. Both are thinking of the disaster which had almost overtaken Glimville.

Behind them, they leave the Glimville Bagelunculus, stiff, stale, and harmless.

Or is it?